water

wet

work

Phonics Friends

Wan and the Dog Wash
The Sound of W

The
**Child's
World**

By Joanne Meier and Cecilia Minden

E
PHONICS
MEIER

Id's
•rld

in the United States of America
nild's World®
PO Box 326
Chanhassen, MN 55317-0326
800-599-READ
www.childsworld.com

A special thank you to Diane's Dog Grooming shop and the Jarema family for allowing "Murphy" to be washed in public, and to Sarah for tackling such a big job.

The Child's World®: Mary Berendes, Publishing Director

Editorial Directions, Inc.: E. Russell Primm, Editorial Director and Project Editor; Katie Marsico, Associate Editor; Judith Shiffer, Associate Editor and School Media Specialist; Linda S. Koutris, Photo Researcher and Selector

The Design Lab: Kathleen Petelinsek, Design and Page Production

Photographs ©: Photo setting and photography by Romie and Alice Flanagan/Flanagan Publishing Services.

Library of Congress Cataloging-in-Publication Data
Meier, Joanne D.
  Wan and the dog wash : the sound of W / by Joanne Meier and Cecilia Minden.
     p. cm. — (Phonics friends)
  Summary: Simple text featuring the sound of the letter "w" describes a child washing a dog.
  ISBN 1-59296-308-0 (library bound : alk. paper)
  [1. English language—Phonetics. 2. Reading.] I. Minden, Cecilia. II. Title. III. Series.
  PZ7.M5148Wan 2004
  [E]—dc22   2004003543

Note to parents and educators:
The Child's World® has created Phonics Friends with the goal of exposing children to engaging stories and pictures that assist in phonics development. The books in the series will help children learn the relationships between the letters of written language and the individual sounds of spoken language. This contact helps children learn to use these relationships to read and write words.

The books in this series follow a similar format. An introductory page, to be read by an adult, introduces the child to the phonics feature, or sound, that will be highlighted in the book. Read this page to the child, stressing the phonic feature. Help the student learn how to form the sound with her mouth. The Phonics Friends story and engaging photographs follow the introduction. At the end of the story, word lists categorize the feature words into their phonic element. Additional information on using these lists is on The Child's World® Web site listed at the top of this page.

Each book in this series has been carefully written to meet specific readability requirements. Close attention has been paid to elements such as word count, sentence length, and vocabulary. Readability formulas measure the ease with which the text can be read and understood. Each Phonics Friends book has been analyzed using the Spache readability formula. For more information on this formula, as well as the levels for each of the books in this series please visit The Child's World® Web site.

Reading research suggests that systematic phonics instruction can greatly improve students' word recognition, spelling, and comprehension skills. The Phonics Friends series assists in the teaching of phonics by providing students with important opportunities to apply their knowledge of phonics as they read words, sentences, and text.

This is the letter *w.*

In this book, you will read words that have the *w* sound as in:

wash, wet, water, and *work.*

Wan has a big job.

She has to wash her dog Wags.

First, Wan gets Wags all

wet. She uses warm water.

Wan washes Wags.

Wags likes the warm water.

Wan wishes Wags would stand still. This is hard work!

Wan gets the soap.

She washes the dog well.

Wan uses more water. She

makes sure the water is warm.

Wan is done.

Wags is clean and wet!

Wan wants to dry Wags.

She gets a warm towel.

Oh no! Wags shakes and shakes. Now Wags and Wan are both wet!

Fun Facts

Water makes up most of our planet and plays a very important part in our lives. If you think of earth as a giant pie with ten pieces, eight of those pieces would represent the portion of earth's surface that is made up of water. Of those eight pieces, less than one would represent the amount of water that is safe for drinking. The rest is seawater or water that is frozen in glaciers.

Perhaps you don't have a job right now, but you probably would if you lived in the 1800s. Children worked in mines, factories, farms, and stores. They picked cotton, shined shoes, sold newspapers, canned fish, made clothes, and wove fabric. They usually worked twelve hours a day, seven days a week. So the next time your mom asks you to take out the garbage, smile and be happy you weren't born a hundred years ago!

Activity

Performing an Experiment with Water

Fill a glass with water until it is completely full. Next, drop one coin into the water. Slowly add another, and then another. You will probably start to notice that the surface of the water becomes more and more rounded. The water is allowing the surface to stretch before it breaks and the water overflows. See how many coins it takes before the water overflows.

To Learn More

Books
About the Sound of W
Flanagan, Alice K. *Wish and Win: The Sound of W.* Chanhassen, Minn.: The Child's World, 2000.

About Water
Base, Graeme. *The Water Hole.* New York: Harry N. Abrams, 2001.
Dodd, Dayle Ann, and Tor Freeman (illustrator). *Pet Wash.* Cambridge, Mass.: Candlewick Press, 2001.
Wick, Walter. *A Drop of Water: A Book of Science and Wonder.* New York: Scholastic, 1997.

About Work
Bunting, Eve, and Ronald Himler (illustrator). *A Day's Work.* New York: Clarion Books, 1994.
Parish, Peggy, and Lynn Sweat (illustrator). *Good Work, Amelia Bedelia.* New York: Greenwillow Books, 1976.
Williams, Sherley Anne, and Carole Byard (illustrator). *Working Cotton.* San Diego: Harcourt Brace Jovanovich, 1992.

Web Sites
Visit our home page for lots of links about the Sound of W:

http://www.childsworld.com/links.html

Note to Parents, Teachers, and Librarians: We routinely check our Web links to make sure they're safe, active sites—so encourage your readers to check them out!

W Feature Words

Proper Names

Wags

Wan

Feature Words in Initial Position

want

warm

wash

water

well

wet

wish

work

would

About the Authors

Joanne Meier, PhD, has worked as an elementary school teacher and university professor. She earned her BA in early childhood education from the University of South Carolina, and her MEd and PhD in education from the University of Virginia. She currently works as a literacy consultant for schools and private organizations. Joanne Meier lives with her husband Eric, and spends most of her time chasing her two daughters, Kella and Erin, and her two cats, Sam and Gilly, in Charlottesville, Virginia.

Cecilia Minden, PhD, directs the Language and Literacy Program at the Harvard Graduate School of Education. She is a reading specialist with classroom and administrative experience in grades K–12. She earned her PhD in reading education from the University of Virginia. Cecilia and her husband Dave Cupp enjoy sharing their love of reading with their granddaughter Chelsea.